To Calvin and Claire, for the brother/sister inspiration.
—A.D.

To my young cousin Wyatt, who—like the early pioneers— has an adventurous spirit.
—T.W.

# To The Top!

## A Gateway Arch Story

*by*

Amanda E Doyle

*Illustrated by* Tony Waters

REEDY PRESS

St. Louis, Missouri

JEFFERSON NATIONAL PARKS ASSOCIATION

"There's the Arch! It's peeking at us!" squealed Jake, craning his neck to see the top of the Gateway Arch over the seat in front of him. "Hold on, Arch, we're coming to the top!"

"Jake," sighed Ella, "the Arch can't hear you . . . and it's not peeking at us, is it Grandpa? It's just standing still."

"Hold on, kids," laughed Grandpa. "You're right, Ella, it's not exactly peeking . . . but it's fun to imagine it's smiling at us, upside down."

"Grandpa, when do we get to the top?" asked Jake.

"Grandpa! I recognize that building! It's the Old Courthouse. We learned about it at school," announced Ella. "Lots of people in pioneer times headed out west from there. Other people went to the Old Courthouse to ask for their rights and freedom."

Jake wished he was old enough to go to school; Ella was always talking about all the things she learned there.

"C'mon, Ella, let's go. We still have to get to the top!" said Jake.

Ella stopped every few steps to take a picture with her new camera.

Finally, they arrived on the grass beneath the Arch. The closer they walked, the bigger it looked, until both Jake and Ella had to bend their heads way, waaaaay back to see the very top.

"Wow!" shouted Jake. "It's so big it's enormous!" Jake liked practicing the big words he heard, and "enormous" was his new favorite.

"Yep," agreed Grandpa. "Can you believe that when your grandpa was a kid, the Arch wasn't even here?"

Both kids stopped and stared at Grandpa.

"What do you mean?" asked Ella.
"Where did it go?" asked Jake.

Grandpa laughed. "The Arch wasn't always here," he explained. "But I sure remember it being built. I was only twelve years old."

"Someone had to *build* it?" asked Ella. "How did they build it? Did it take a long time? You watched them build it? Could we build one? You can't just make a big metal arch out of nothing!" Her questions tumbled out as fast as a waterfall.

"Cool your jets, Ella," said Grandpa. "First, you have to know how it all got started. There was a contest to see who could come up with the best design for a monument to honor the people who expanded our country to the west.

"The winner was a man named Eero Saarinen, and his design was very much like what we see. That shape is called a catenary arch."

Jake thought a caterpillar arch sounded like a pretty funny idea, too.

"So what happened when he won?" asked Ella.

Uh-oh. Jake saw the look Grandpa got when he was going to tell one of his stories. "When are we going to the top?" he asked.

"It took a long time to get the plans just right," Grandpa said. "But in 1963, the first stainless steel piece of the Arch took its spot right here. After that, it seemed like every few weeks there was more and more Arch rising up, until the last piece slid into place more than two years later."

Jake had been walking in circles around Grandpa while he talked. When Jake looked up to the sky, he got so dizzy he almost fell down.

The friendly park ranger nearby helped him get his balance again. "Thanks," said Jake. He added, "I really like your hat!"

"Park rangers work here because the Arch and the ground underneath, and even the Old Courthouse, are part of a national park!" said Ella. Jake interrupted with a loud, "Grandpa!"

Grandpa laughed and said, "Okay, okay; does anyone here want to go to the top?"

"YES!" answered Jake.

"We start our journey to the top by going . . . underneath!" said Grandpa.

Grandpa and the kids left the sunny outdoors and went down, down, down, underneath the ground and the Arch.

Inside the visitor center, Jake noticed a covered wagon and a tipi in the distance, while Ella snapped a photo of Grandpa standing next to a metal man.

"You're almost as tall as the Thomas Jefferson statue," Ella said, "and Jefferson National Expansion Memorial was named after him."

There were so many interesting things to see. The museum told stories of the explorers, pioneers, and traders who left St. Louis and headed out west. Ella had learned all about them at school.

"Grandpa, look at how this chain makes an upside down Arch!" Ella said. "The park ranger said this is a catenary curve, just like the shape of the Arch."

Finally, Grandpa was able to get Jake's attention: "Now, I understand you might be interested in going to the top?"

Jake pulled him all the way to the ticket desk. Then he pulled Grandpa over to wait in line for the tram ride, with Ella trying to keep up.

"Oh, great. Now we have to wait in line,"
moaned Jake. "When do we get to the top?"

But moments later, right before their eyes, he, Ella, and Grandpa saw the doors to their tram car slide open, and they ducked to step inside.

The tram clicked and turned, clicked and turned, as it began its journey to the top of the Arch.

"Are we there yet?" Jake asked.

"Well, we have a four-minute ride to the top," replied Grandpa.

"That's 630 feet up, to be precise," announced Ella. "The Arch is taller than the Washington Monument, taller than the heads on Mount Rushmore, and way taller than the Statue of Liberty!"

Jake wondered how many footballs he would have to stack up to touch the top of the Arch.

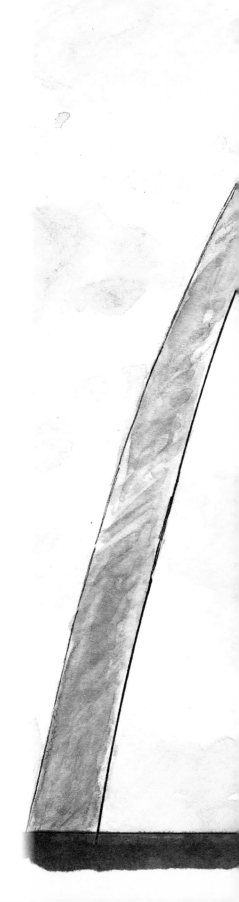

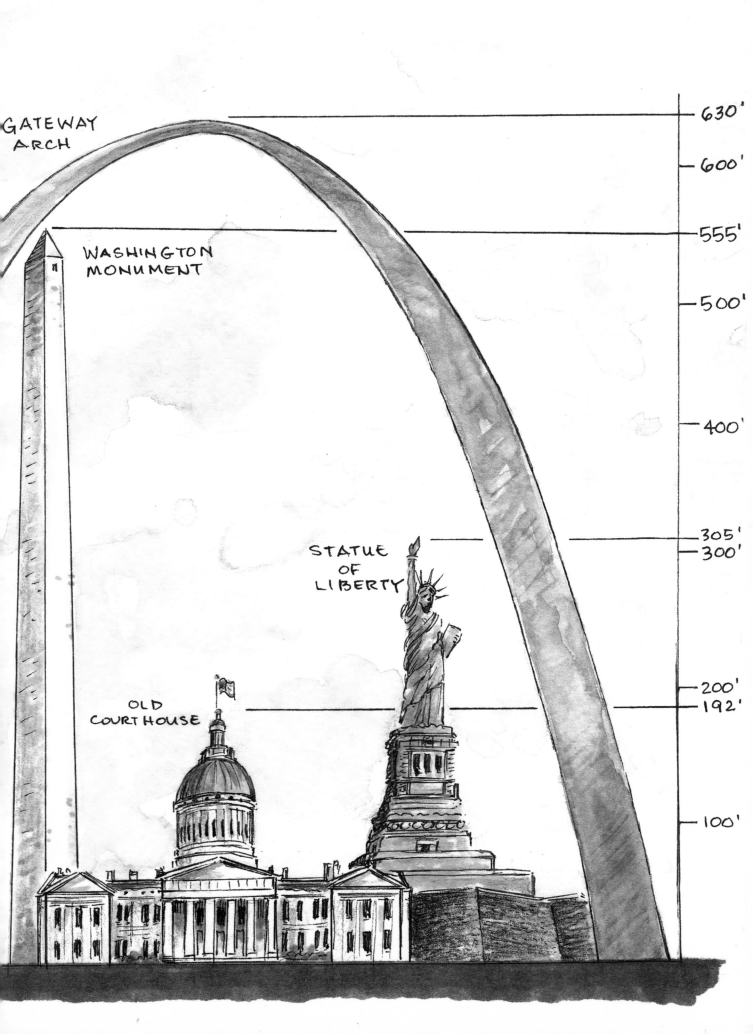

GATEWAY
ARCH

WASHINGTON
MONUMENT

STATUE
OF
LIBERTY

OLD
COURTHOUSE

630'

600'

555'

500'

400'

305'
300'

200'
192'

100'

A few minutes later, the tram slid to a stop. "Hold on kids!" said Grandpa. "Because . . ."

"Grandpa! We made it to the top!" shouted Jake.

"Look at the Mississippi River and all the barges!" said Ella.

Jake, for once, was speechless. But not for long. He gazed at the stadium and the busy city streets below.

"Grandpa?"

"Yes, Jake?"

"When can we go back down there?"

# GATEWAY ARCH
# FUN FACTS

✓ The Gateway Arch is a national park! Its official name is Jefferson National Expansion Memorial. The Old Courthouse is part of the national park, too.

✓ The park is a memorial to President Thomas Jefferson for his role in expanding the West and to Dred Scott, who sued for his freedom at the Old Courthouse. Thomas Jefferson was the third president of the United States.

✓ Construction of the Gateway Arch was completed on October 28, 1965.

✓ The Gateway Arch is 630 feet tall and 630 feet wide.

✓ The tram ride takes 4 minutes to get to the top, but only 3 minutes to get back down.

✓ There are two trams that take people to the top of the Arch. Each tram has 8 capsules, and 5 people can ride in each capsule.

8 x 5 = 40 people

✓ There are 16 windows on each of the 2 sides of the observation room at the top of the Arch.

16 x 2 = 32 windows

✓ The Arch is designed to sway as much as 18 inches in a 150-mile-an-hour wind. But don't be scared! It will only move 1½ inches in a 50-mile-an-hour wind.

✓ The Mississippi River is 2,320 miles long. That's as long as 19,444 Arches sitting side by side!

Reedy Press
PO Box 5131
St. Louis, MO 63139, USA
www.reedypress.com

**Jefferson National Parks Association**
One Memorial Drive, Suite 1900
St. Louis, MO 63102
www.jnpa.com

Library of Congress Control Number: 2012947520

ISBN: 978-1-935806-32-5

Printed in the
United States of America

12 13 14 15 16    5 4 3 2 1